veneficiapublications@gmail.com

Exquisite Sin

Diane Narraway

Contents

Lilith 1

Vampyre 8

The Eternal Kiss.............. 9

Within 13

No Reflection 15

Hungry Soul 16

Follow Me 18

The Ash Tree 20

Countess Erzbet 22

Blood Lust 24

Visitor 26

In Death 27

Music 28

Vows 30

Day and Night 33

Stars 35

Casket 36

My Dream 37

The Kiss 39

Creatures of the Night ... 41

Death's Sweet Lullaby ... 44

My Sweet Love 48

Down Here 50

Deadly Price 53

Whitby Bay 55

My Mother 58

LUCILLE 60

SLAYER 63

DO NOT 64

MEMORIES OF LOVE 65

NOSFERATU 67

PRECIOUS ANGEL 68

YOUR TOUCH 70

SLOWLY 73

MY INCUBUS 74

WILLINGLY 75

TEARS 77

SHADOW 78

REFLECTIONS 79

HELL'S FIRE 81

MY WEEPING HEART 82

SHADOW ON THE WALL 85

LOVE 88

GRIEF 90

SENSES 93

DAMNED 96

INTRODUCTION

This book is written for all those who fell in love with the gothic Vampyre. Those individuals who devoured Bram Stoker and Polidori, and who flock to watch the latest retelling of Dracula, or any other Vampyre movie.

The Vampyre began as something to be feared: the medieval revenant, the Nosferatu, the undead, who sought out and preyed on the living, condemning them to suffer the same fate. They were unholy beasts, ugly and deformed, born at a time when the process of decay that followed death was not yet understood.

It is possible that a man known as Jure Grando was the first account of a real person being considered undead. In 1656, in the small town of Kringa, in the Istrian peninsula near Tinjan, Jure Grando died of an illness. However, local legend claimed that he rose from the grave and returned to the town each night.

1

Locally he was referred to as a Vampyre (štrigon), who is said to have terrorised the village until 1672, when his grave was opened, and his corpse decapitated.

The succubus and incubus too have their home amongst these fearsome repugnant creatures. However, unlike the bloodthirsty revenant, they seduced their victims to death!

The succubus being the feminine and the incubus, their masculine counterpart, were demons that visited their victims in the night. It is believed that the victims were intended to parent their unholy offspring. The earliest account of one of these attacks' dates back to around 2100 BCE and can be found in the epic of Gilgamesh.

The story tells how the incubus, which in this instance is Gilgamesh's father Lilu, interfered with women while they slept. It appears Lilu was not the only incubus as the passage mentions several of these vampiric spirits; wicked daemon Utukku who slays man alive on the plain, the vengeful spirit Alû who covers (man) like a garment, the wraith Etimmu who binds the body, Lilu the nightbird/spirit who wanders in the plain. There is also mention of another spirit, the Lammea (Lamme/Lamashtu), who causes disease to those he encounters.

Gilgamesh goes on to tell how these beings have come to cause suffering to mankind, by way of a 'painful malady' in his body.

This account comes from around the same time that Lilitu, or Lilith first made an appearance as the incubus' female counterpart, the succubus who allegedly frequented the erotic dreams of unsuspecting males.

According to Jewish folklore, Lilith is made at the same time, and from the same dirt as Adam. Unlike Eve, who is made from his rib, Lilith considers herself Adam's equal. In some accounts she leaves him and the Garden of Eden in temper, while in others she is banished. Regardless of which version you believe, Lilith leaves Eden and mates with the archangel Samael. As a result,

Yahweh rendered her unable to have children and so, she either walked the Earth stealing children from their cribs, or seducing men in a vain attempt to produce a child.

These nightly seductions, or attacks, resulted in the victim being gradually drained of their lifeforce. Their early symptoms closely resembled those of a Vampyre victim: pallid skin, loss of weight, and dark sunken eyes.

In some accounts the children of the incubus are deformed, and or sickly. This possibly had more to do with a lack of medical understanding or knowledge of the effects caused by inbreeding.

There is a mythical creature known as the Manananggal in Phillipine folklore. With its bat-like wings, claws, and fangs it could easily be considered an early ancestor of the modern vampire.

The majority of Manananggals are female, with the power to split their bodies in two. The upper torso takes flight during the night in search of human prey. Allegedly their preferred victims are pregnant women. The Mananangals long tongue enters the woman, in order to suck the blood and heart from the unborn baby. The lower torso remains on the ground, and is, due to its inability to move, the more vulnerable of the two halves.

It is said that sprinkling salt, smearing crushed garlic, or ash on top of the grounded torso is fatal to the creature. If this occurs, then the upper torso would not be able to reconnect to itself. As a result, it would perish at sunrise.

There is some argument for the Egyptian goddess Sekhmet being a Vampyre. Sekhmet was the warrior goddess of death and healing. Her father, Ra, the god of the sun god and creator of mankind, sent his daughter to punish man.

This very much parallels the biblical flood, minus the rain of course, where Yahweh punishes mankind for their disloyalty to their god as well as their wicked behaviour. Ra, like Yahweh effectively sent Sekhmet to rain slaughter upon the human race, and as she did so, she drank their blood to gain power.

It was, possibly still is, an accepted practice to drink the blood, or even eat the flesh of the vanquished or the revered to gain their power.

This introduction wouldn't be complete without a mention of those driven by a darker bloodlust.

Countess Elizabeth Bathory was said to bathe in the blood of virgin girls to retain her youthful looks. It is claimed that a local sorceress had given her an incantation, which she recited in the mirror before draining the blood of her victims. Initially, it is believed that she used aristocratic girls, but when questions started being asked she used local peasant and serving girls.

Voivode Vladimir Dracul – whose surname translates to Son of the Dragon was the ruler of Wallachia three times between 1448 and his death in 1476/77. Despite his penchant for impaling his enemies, which earned him the name Vlad the Impaler, he is still considered one of the most important rulers in Wallachian history and a Romanian national hero. He is reputed to have taken meals sat in in his garden surrounded by impaled corpses.

There is some suggestion that Elizabeth Bathory and Vlad the Impaler possibly had their ancestral roots in the same order of the Dragon.

Whatever the cause, along with the seductive allure of the incubus and succubus, they were compelling enough to inspire writers, poets, and artists. This resulted in the gothic Vampyre, born into an era of the romantic and the libertine. Polidori's Lord Ruthven was created in a world of poets, and high society. It is easy to see how the Vampyre became part of the gentry. Likewise, Bram Stoker's Dracula draws upon the legendary Voivode Vlad III Dracul.

The poems in this collection are inspired by Polidori, Bram Stoker and Shakespeare, with some dalliances involving the darker side of blood lust. I am grateful to all those poets, writers, film makers and artists, without whom this book would not be possible.

Lilith

Buried deep within the void
Where everything and nothing,
Silently waits to be destroyed,
Heralding her new beginning.

And in the cold dark nothingness
Destruction and creation flow,
With effervescent easiness
As her light begins to show.

A swirling mass of matter
That spews forth new-born stars -
An energy that rips and shatters
In chaos unsurpassed.

Yet somehow there lies within
A beauty and a peace,
Bringing with it guilt and sin
A universal beast.

And when the fury did subside
And peace at last was heard,
The Light and Truth could then
divide
And wisdom became the Word.

By divine hand was night and day,
As the world was taking form,
The vault of heaven over waters lay
On that primordial dawn.

Her beauty and her serenity
Demanded that time obeyed,
Whilst overshadowed, by the trinity
The land and seas were made.

And when she saw the origins of life
First crawl upon the Earth,
Pre -destined to be Adams wife,
So long before his birth.

Through time and space still yet
infernal
To create a paradise,
A beauty and a love so eternal
With divine truth so wise.

Seasons that would come and go
Ruled by the moon and sun.
The mysterious ebb and flow,
Signed by the purest one.

Then every living creature is driven,
To a partner of its kind,
For man and woman, love is given,
With power of the mind.

While through Zion ran the river
Styx
To then divide and flow,

Into the land of gold and onyx,
Four separate ways to go.

The garden there beyond compare
Built towards the east,
Precious virgin. Eden fair,
The land that named the beast.

The light which shone so feminine
Watched Adam from the heart,
Knowing that to be with him
Meant they could never part.

Then with all heavenly consent
And given as a gift,
Transcending all earthly intent
Celestial. Seductive, Lilith.

Unlike Gilgamesh who there before
Had sought eternal youth,

Adam with angelic whore
Walked within the truth.

Taking Adam to be with her
At the setting of the sun,
Until the rising of the stars
They became as one.

That light from deep within the void
Long before the birth of time,
Love so true she soon destroyed
A sensual adversary so sublime.

Then in anger and in haste,
Shapeshifting she took flight.
Fallen from his grace,
Lilith so contrite.

The way to Adam now lies barred
By sword and cherubim,

While Lilith now bruised, and scarred,
Knows another lies with him.

Maligned by those who disbelieve,
Scorned by those who do,
The biblical, temptress Eve,
Now Adams wife so true.

Formed from his flesh and bone,
Submissive and puerile,
Seduced by serpent while alone
In treachery so vile.

And while Adam succumbed to his mate,
What twisted perverse reason,
Allows forbidden fruit to be ate,
As angel falls to demon.

Punished Eve still takes her place,
As the mother of mankind.
While Lilith who fell from grace
None shall ever find.

Judged and sentenced without trial
Goddess of the storm,
Abandoned, cold, and sterile,
Goddess, lost upon the dawn.

How ignorant. How inhumane,
To perpetuate the myth,
And scorn the beauty and the pain
Of the light once known as Lilith.

VAMPYRE

Black roses and lace,
Promise exquisite sin,
As the sweet scent of death
Stirs something within.

And while Cerberus guards
The door to my heart,
My satanic lust
Tears you apart.

As my soul drips with blood,
I watch yours burn like fire.
As you want ...
                    Need ...
                              Hunger for ...

The kiss of the Vampyre.

The Eternal Kiss

Dark Graveyard wherein lies
An ancient altar made of stone.
Draped upon this night,
As shadows dance,
In full moonlight
Dressed in animal skins and bone.

I lie in wait, arched naked
For my lover to appear:
To heed the call of my heart,
Hips slightly raised,
And legs apart,
I tremble, both with lust and fear.

I sense your presence here,
And feel your demonic breath,
As your lips brush against my skin.

Feel my faint heart,
That beats within,
For it longs to conquer death.

I hunger for the power,
Hidden in the fivefold kiss.
Obscene and highly potent,
I'm the willing prey,
In this wild hunt:
In this savage, deadly tryst.

So, linger softly with each kiss
Slowly upwards to my breasts,
Growing ever more intense,
In passionate recompense.
Taking me to greater heights,
And my soul to greater depths.

Fill me with all you are,
Satisfy my growing lust.
Between my thighs,
Deep inside,
Writhing in pure delight,
With every pulsing thrust.

My body heaves with desire
For this demon of the night,
Whose love is cold,
Yet burns my soul,
In his erotic embrace,
I long to be his bride.

I'm powerless in his arms.
His touch, his breath,
They make me sigh,
Sending shivers down my spine.
My fingernails rip his skin,
As I draw closer to my death.

The last deadly kiss upon my lips
Makes my body burn like fire,
And when he is done,
My blood shall run,
In sweet surrender
to the Vampyre.

WITHIN

Within the mirrors of time now lost
Hides all that I've become.
I, the beauty, and the beast,
To which you shall succumb.

Within the blood of ages past,
Lies all the futures dreams,
And all that you shall ever be
Is hidden in your screams.

Within the lies of days gone by,
Waits a truth to be awoken,
I, the creature in the dark
Will mend the heart that's broken.

Within the veins of hopes, and fears
Lies the lover's potent kiss.
I, your darkness, and your light,
Will bring you euphoria and bliss.

Within the sorrow of your soul,
Awakes, a hunger and a need,
You, eternal, just like me,
Will long to see another bleed.

No Reflection

No reflection,
Unsatiated lust,
Nothing but hunger,
Hope turned to dust.

Unsatiated lust,
A greed unsurpassed,
Only my desire
Destined to last.

Nothing but hunger
Which remains unfulfilled.
The constant yearning
For the blood I have spilled.

Hope turned to dust
All that remains is despair,
The hollow remains
Of a soul unable to care.

Hungry Soul

I watch you in the wintry night,
Hidden in the dark.
The faint streetlight,
flickering on your pale skin.
I see the emptiness
The hungry soul that lies within.

And I wonder what you need,
A wife, a mistress?
A priestess or a witch?
A mother, a whore,
An actor, a piper,
Or simply a bitch?

How many will seek to inspire?
Some through their wisdom
Others through desire.
Each one playing their part,
calling the tune,
And summoning the heart.

So, what is it that you seek?
Art, poetry, music,
Religion, romance
Magick, mystery, science,
Or a place in life's dance?

Could it be me that will feed,
The ravenous hunger that lies
Deep in your soul?
Yet reflects in your eyes,
As the faint street light flickers
Upon your pale skin,
You remain ravenous and raw,
Searching for what satisfies.

FOLLOW ME

Follow me, Come follow me,
For I see your desire burns,
and I can feel your eyes upon me,
Follow me,
Follow me, Come follow me.

Through star kissed woods
to a moonlit world,
beneath the devil's tree.
Follow me,
Follow me, Come follow me.

Where darkness rules,
the icy heart, and death
will our secrets keep.
Follow me,
Follow me, Come follow me.

Through the ensuing
timeless years, as we
walk the blood-soaked streets.
Follow me,
Follow me, come follow me.

And taste the kiss,
that sweetly lingers as it
melts away your fears.
Follow me.
Follow me, come follow me.

THE ASH TREE

Is there another
Who could love you more,
down there, where you lie
All the seasons through?

Is there another,
one you find more fair?
Laid in your grave with you,
Who'll be forever true?

Is death's kiss
A more passionate kiss,
Than mine could ever be. –
A kiss for all eternity?

Is the Vampyre's love,
A more powerful love.
than ever you had with me,
Beneath this old Ash tree?

Does immortality bind you,
In some way are you charmed?
Are the words of my prayer,
A sweet and hollow whisper?

What is it that holds you
Down there among the dead?
When I am cursed to never sleep,
And in dread silence softly weep?

I know mines a love that's lost
And your soul is hungry still?
But I'll treasure it both night and
day
While 'neath the Ash Tree you are
laid.

Countess Erzbet

Child that danced naked,
With the morning star,
The accuser alone,
Knows who you are.

The childhood bride,
Of the heroic knight,
But forbidden lust
Was your true delight.

So, when hell offered up
Its prize bitch whore,
You accepted her love,
Then begged her for more.

Consumed by the desire,
Of a love so depraved,

Meant torture and bloodshed,
Was all that you craved.

Murdering the pure,
With un-justified rage,
To bathe in their blood,
Thus, preventing old age.

But when the carnivals over,
And the whore burns in hell,
The love that you shared,
Will be your prison cell.

Heartbroken and haggard,
Old bent and frail,
You're the evil vain queen,
In a child's fairy tale.

Blood Lust

On the streets of London
Watching the maiden fair,
Who knows what wretched thoughts
and deeds,
Run through your tainted mind,
While skulking in your lair?

The venom surging through your
veins
Poisons all you sense.
And those poor few that knew your
name,
In the darkest alleyways
Knew a love so intense.

And like a well-cut suit you wear
Such an elegant disdain
The shadow that stalks the street,

With a tortured heart
And a hunger to sustain.

Yet the stench of sweat and fear
Somehow so pure and feminine.
Your conscience eased,
By the flowing blood
That cleanses them from sin.

Burning deep inside your soul
A void that can't be filled,
Until the last breath leaves
The one you so desire,
And no more blood is spilled.

Visitor

Across the corridors of time
Your scent disturbs my sleep,
From within the astral haze
Visiting my darkest dreams.

Satiate my scarlet lust
In the shadows of the moon,
Where every single heartbeat
Whispers an ancient truth.

For though I partake of this world
In all its earthy delight,
Nothing stills my restless soul
Like the visitor of the night.

In Death

White and pallid flawless skin.
Ashen and cold,
Is the heart,
That so faintly beats within.
Your lips, now, so pale and dry,
Once beautiful
And cherished,
By so many, shall soon be mine.
I wait solely for your last breath
To take you
To my heart
And walk beside you in death
So, take the hand of eternal youth
Love and live
By my side
In a purer, darker truth.

Music

If music be the food of love, play on.
Bring symphony to my ear,
Until the stars burn out above.

If theatre be the food of lust, act out.
Bring drama to the stage of life,
'Til soliloquy turns to dust.

If art be the food of hope, paint bold.
Bring colour to my loneliness
Until my story has been told.

If dance be the food of dreams, sleep
deep.
Bring shape to my darkest night
Until I can learn to weep.

*If pain be the food of sorrow, then
bleed.
Bring meaning to this anguish
Until I can feel once more.*

*If word be the food of the soul, then
pray.
Bring light into this empty heart
Until the break of day.*

---

1 Opening line from Twelfth Night – William Shakespeare

Vows

Would that I were ever yours alone
Sweet Vampyre of the night,
Would that I could dare to wish,
To linger by your throne.
Would that I could ever be,
Yours until the end of time.
Would that I could ever hope,
To be your only lawful bride.

For I, would take thee to be
My lawful wedded husband.
Signed and sealed for all to see,
With a precious golden band.
I would promise to have, and to hold
You forever close to me.
From this day forward for better,
And for worse, and that which lies
between.

Should all our riches turn to ash,
And upon hard times we fall,
Or if our health should fail
And sickness come to call,
I'll be there to love and cherish
Every single night and day.
And whatever you should ask of me,
Then surely I will obey.

And I would sing unto the heavens
Loud and clear, and from the heart,
With almighty God's holy laws
Till death do us part.
But I can only ever dream,
Oh, beautiful revenant,
For you defy the laws of nature
And the holy sacrament.

But would that it could ever be,
I would break those holy laws.
And declare my undying love
To be forever yours
And I know that its forbidden
An abomination and a sin.
But just for tonight my love,
Sweet Vampyre I invite you in.

Day and Night

You are day,
I am the night,
Your skin flushed pink,
Mine translucent white.

Your lips full and plump,
Mine pale and thin,
Your eyes are bright,
Mine are hollow, sunken in.
I yearn for your beauty
Yet you detest my face,
Your life is charmed,
Mine is a disgrace.

The candle flame flickers
Beside your bed,
While I hide in the shadows
And walk with the dead.

But just whisper the words
And invite me in.
One taste of your blood,
And you'll walk in sin,
Reach out to me,
Call my name,
Take my hand,
Share my pain.

Stars

The stars align,
The clock strikes twelve,
And midnight wraps me
In her velvet love.

Sweet Nut, she dances
By my side this night,
Holds close my tortured soul,
And caresses my twisted heart.

Lady Luna, lights the path
That I must travel along,
In silver mist she walks with me
And gently holds my hand.

But in the twilight dawn,
When the morning star shines bright.
I will turn my face away
And vanish in the shade.

Casket

Enveloped in silk,
Your family surround you,
Weeping for their loss:
Their loss, my gain.
Their sorrow, my joy,
Their despair, my hope.

Upon your casket,
Are placed flowers and bows:
To reflect your beauty,
Their beauty, my love,
Their daughter, my bride,
Their grief, my delight.

Ashes to Ashes,
And from dust to dust,
They say their goodbyes:
Their goodbye, my hello
Their farewell, my forever,
Their heartbreak, my Vampyre.

My Dream

In my dream
I can be,
All that you want,
All that you think you need.
But I will
drive you insane,
and leave your heart to bleed.

I am the
sweetest rose,
with the sharpest thorns,
That promises
True love,
Yet brings nothing but scorn.

For a while,
I could even
be your perfect mate

Draped upon your arm.
But it is
An illusion
That will only cause you harm.

But no matter
The cost,
You will follow me still,
And hang on my every word.
Open your,
Veins until
I've drunk my fill.

Then in death
You will rise,
And walk at my side,
Another beautiful Mortal.
Destined
To become
Just one of my brides.

THE KISS

One kiss from me,
Upon thy feet,
Transcends the thresholds of all
time,
And the words I speak,
Are bittersweet,
As I yearn to make you mine.

Then shiver as I
Kiss thy knees,
For they shall kneel before the gate,
Where the soul takes flight,
Beyond the light
And surrenders to its fate.

Yield to me as I,
Kiss thy phallus,
Taking you to realms as yet unseen,

For within the bliss,
Of this erotic kiss,
I'm all there has ever been.

I place a kiss,
Upon thy chest,
Which guards thy faintly beating
heart,
And as I drink my fill,
Thy heart grows still,
Turning the world from light to dark.

My final kiss,
Is upon thy lips,
Sealing all that is yet to come,
And demons sleep,
While angels weep,
As with thy last breath my will is
done.

CREATURES OF THE NIGHT

Ivy twists around a marker
Celtic in origin,
A lone crow calls on high,
As darkness closes in.

The world seems lost in time,
Dark clouds cross the moon,
Shadows dance in the dusk
To an unfamiliar tune.

A desperate longing fills the air,
The sense of love long gone,
An unyielding hopelessness,
Of a time lost upon the dawn.

A sad and sorrowful lament,
Fills the cool night air,

And amid the swirling mist
Hope turns to despair.

The creatures of the night
Rise from their eternal sleep,
And through hallowed ground,
Softly, in silence creep.

A screech owl screams,
Trees whisper to the breeze,
Cobwebs shimmer in the half light,
And the devil never sleeps.

When the world lays still
On a cold wintry night,
The land of silvery frost
And nightmares comes alive.

Tread soft and swift,
For this is no more than an illusion.
The realm of half-light, and halfling,
Is a world of dark collusion.

Here love is dark and powerful,
Something primitive and cold,
Whose touch is a bitter curse
That destroys a mortal soul.

Death's Sweet Lullaby

Would that I could write such words
I'd etch them deep upon my soul,
For such words of love are more
valuable
Than silver, gems, or gold.

But my words and soul are tainted,
Tinged with pain and sorrow,
And the words of love I speak
Are bitter, cold, and hollow.

My world is dark and lonely
Devoid of light, I tread in shade.
It lies betwixt the river Styx
And Hades; the Elysian Parade.

Once where beauty trod carefree
There is only spite and scorn,
And lovers whose kisses I once
tasted,
Are lost in the twilight of the dawn.

But words of love turned to dust
Still linger upon my tongue,
Bringing thoughts of desire once felt,
A long-forgotten song, once sung.

Such sad words can't be portrayed
In a thousand lines or more,
Instead, they fly upon the winds
Shallow even to the core.

Drunk, intoxicated, delirious;
Bereft of all humane desire,
Sunken to the depths of hell,
My soul, my heart, afire.

I bleed for those who cross my path,
Taste their misery, feel their pain.
Cast aside their hopelessness,
Temptation alone shall be their
bane.

Within my eyes, look deep poor fool,
Reflections of your despair, your
lust,
For my beautiful, wretched lover
Misplaced is your sweet trust.

Discarded, as old and wretched hag,
Left to wither in the early sunlight.
Love's first deadly kiss,
Steals a life of promise and delight.

Upon reflection, how I've sinned
As Eve did with just one bite.

*Condemned so many to ash and
bone,
With every step death following
behind.*

*Pierce my breast, deep into my
heart,
That I may breathe my last,
And sit at the table of the damned,
A bittersweet reminder, of a loveless
past.*

*So, sing me sweetly to my fate,
Wrapp'd in all the tears I've cried,
Lamenting lovers lost along the way,
Yet all fades with death's sweet
lullaby.*

My Sweet Love

Dearest, darling, my sweet love,
I long for your embrace,
Every night I wait for you
Dressed in silk and lace.

Without you the world is dark,
The days blend into one,
Wine it seems my only friend,
As the weeks roll into months.

Must I cry a thousand tears,
Or die a thousand times?
Broken hearted, all alone,
Sentenced without crime.

I beg you please return to me,
Come to my bed this night.

Kiss me as you have before,
Your touch is my delight.

Oh, my love, my incubus,
Sweet demon dressed in sin,
Come knock upon my window,
Let me, invite you in.

Down Here

I can feel you reach for me
Down here beneath the ground,
I can feel you reaching out
But I can never touch your hand.
I can hear you call to me,
Down here where I sleep.
I can hear you call my name,
But I can never, ever speak.

I can sense you by my side
Down here where I am lay.
I can sense you every night
But I can never feel your pain.
I can know your grieving heart
Down here where I lay still.
I can know your heart is broken,
But I can never help it heal.

I can remember your desire
Down here dressed in silk and lace.
I can remember your lust,
But I can nevermore fill that space.
I can feel the thorny roses
Down here where I'm alone.

I can feel them pierce my heart
But I can never smell their scent.
I can feel the wooden stake
Down here piercing my breast,
And I can hear your faint goodbye
But I can never truly rest.

I can hear you walk away
Down here within my grave.
I can hear you faintly sob,
But I can never leave this place.

I can scream and shout farewell
Down here where I'll remain.
I can scream, and curse aloud,
But you will never hear me again.

A Deadly Price

Blazing red and orange streaks
flash across the sky,
As the sun slowly descends
And Hesperus brings the night.

Creatures beyond our realm
Now walk upon the land;
In the twilight of the dusk
They gently take your hand.

Wonder, at their delicacy
Their beauty and allure;
The darkness in their eyes
Chills, you to the core.

Long fingers beckon you
Into their world of death;

Promises of eternal youth
Dripping softly from their breath.

Their smile captivates and charms,
Yet theirs a deadly kiss,
With lips, plump and bloody-red
They offer a tantalising glimpse.

Theirs is a life of horror and pain,
A life of unending death and decay,
Immortality and youth at a deadly
price,
But is it one you're willing to pay?

WHITBY BAY

Across the ocean deep and harsh
To where you, sleeping lay,
Across the ocean deep and harsh
To where you, my true love waits.

An eerie mist shrouded the ship
From the moment it left Port,
An eerie mist shrouded the ship
With the moon my only consort.

Cold winds tore and ripp'd the sails;
The fog hid the bloody carnage,
Cold winds tore and ripp'd the sails
Throughout this ill-fated passage.

Violence wrenched this crew apart
Whose voices the ghostly cries?
Violence wrenched this crew apart
Such was their last goodbyes.

And lo, what madness lingered
Upon those mighty savage waves,
And lo, what madness lingered
Dragging so many to their graves.

Demeter toss'd upon dark on cold
water
All her crew plunged into the deep,
Demeter toss'd upon dark cold
water
While all the while you sleep.

I have travelled many long harsh
months
To this strange and wondrous land.
I have travelled many long harsh
months
With my cargo of earth and silver
sand.

Oh, how I endured the roughest seas
As the storm raged night and day,
Oh, how I endured the roughest seas
To find you here, in Whitby Bay.

My Mother

My mother's milk,
the fresh blood
of angels while they sleep.

My mother's touch,
gentle and she
alone my soul doth keep.

My mother's kiss,
a curse upon my lips,
like the secrets I must keep.

My mother's hand, so soft,
yet cold to the touch,
her blood runs thick and deep.

My mother's love,
haunts the dark
of all my waking dreams.

My mother's tears
are cold as ice,
as for her child she softly weeps.

Lucille

Before Lucille
there was nothing,
an empty abyss
devoid of any true meaning.
I walked the streets,
in the shadows I hid my face,
and drank the blood of those
dressed in linen and Chantilly lace.
But from somewhere in the dark
came Lucille pure and fair,
with cheeks flushed red,
all framed in a crown of golden hair.

Such beaty I could not leave,
for another less honourable than I,
so, I drank my fill and walked with
Lucille into the night, her forever at
my side.

Oh, but forever is an age or more
and love grows stale with time,
and so, I left Lucille to the mercy
of both gods and man,
One dark and lonely night.

My one regret my fair love, my own
Lucille
for all the tears I've cried,
was how I left you alone to such a
fate,
on a road devoid
of either love or grace.

Oh, how I screamed upon that night
when I heard them pierce your
heart;
forevermore should I walk in shame
in memory of Lucille,
the light within the dark.

Yet I cannot bear such heartache,
the anguish and such painful sorrow,
so tonight, I will quench my thirst,
and watch the sun come up
tomorrow.

Slayer

Garlic wearing, muscle bound,
Cross bearing, stands his ground,
God fearing, powerful, and proud,
Crucifix slinging, for the crowd.
Stake wielding, shouting loud,
Watch me pleading, hear my vows,
My heart bleeding, dust all around,
Van Helsing, pious, and devout.

Do Not

You should run far from me;
Do you not see how I am cursed?
You should turn and hide away,
For, I am followed by hoof and
hearse.
You should leave 'ere nightfall
As mine is a dangerous lust,
Court old age, so thy body turns
to ash and thy bones to dust.
Do not seek to join my world
For it is filled with shadow,
Eternal darkness of the heart
Such longing. Oh, such sorrow.
Run far towards the sunrise,
With open arms greet the early
dawn,
Forget thy sanguine desires
In the twilight of the morn.

MEMORIES OF LOVE

I remember the sunlit sky,
the taste of wine upon my lips,
my sweetheart beneath the tree:
Its leaves shading her from
the sweltering noonday sun.

I remember moonlit walks
The taste of her kiss upon my lips
And how gaslit lamps
lit our way on eerie,
on darker, new moon nights.

I remember the bedside light
And the touch of her fingertips,
The scent of my sweetheart
so soft to the touch, as I held
Her through the night.

I remember the blazing firelight
And how the shadows would skip
around the parlour walls.
cast by dancing flames as they
pirouetted in the hearth.

I remember too, the fateful night
My sweetheart from me was ripp'd.
Within the hidden realms
of hell lies my broken heart,
Still beating softly in the dark.

Nosferatu

Monster, revenant,
Creature of the night,
Hungry, thirsty,
Yearning for a bite.
Incubus, succubus,
Demon in the shadow,
Whose lust is ravenous,
yet empty and hollow.
Foul devil, evil ghoul,
Spirit in the dark,
Whisper Nosferatu,
the keeper of my heart.
For the beautiful, beast
That calls to my soul,
Each, and every night,
Is all that makes me whole.

PRECIOUS ANGEL

Sleep, my precious angel sleep
For soon you shall arise,
And see the world renewed,
Through deep rose-tinted eyes.

Dance, my precious angel dance,
Bewitching is the danse macabre,
Wild is the night, harken, my angel
To the creatures of Proserpina.

Live, my precious angel live,
For eternal youth is ours,
Our beauty will endure forever
As we share these precious hours.

Lust, my precious angel lust,
After all that you desire,

Feed your ravenous hunger
As your soul burns like fire.

Oh, but weep, my precious angel
weep,
For all that you have left behind,
Wonder at why you let it go
To love a stranger lost in time.

YOUR TOUCH

The stench of graveyards
on your breath,
A heavy, earthy, yet
distinctive perfume,
Though I am locked
in an unnatural sleep,
I sense your ghostly presence
in my room,

I feel your touch,
it burns deep in my soul,
And the pain lingers long
after you are gone.
Your kiss leaves me
hopeless, breathless,
Aching, wanting,
and longing for someone,

And I see in your eyes
how death follows you,
Where're you go,
its trail lies in your wake.
I can hear my heart,
as it softly beats
As in your presence,
it's growing ever faint.

I have known you
through the centuries:
Your touch, your scent,
your lust, your grace,
and in the dark,
your hunger and embrace.

Oh, I would walk for all
the aeons yet to come,
If you would walk
with me by my side,

Forever and a day,
for all the endless years,
Forever and a day,
if I could be your bride.

Slowly

Soft are the whispers,
Of love declared after dark;
The twilight moments of love,
A forbidden spark.

Many are the tears,
On my pillow at daybreak,
As is the empty chasm within,
That brings me such heartache.

Shallow is my breath
When you are around,
And I yearn for moments,
Peaceful and profound.

Now I see death's shadow
Cast upon the wall,
How willingly I accept my fate
And succumb to his call.

My Incubus

While my spouse lay by my side
Sleeping deep and sound,
That's when my incubus
comes quietly creeping round.

His touch makes me shiver
And tingle with delight.
Oh, how he does love me
All through the longest night.

Yet in the cold light of day
All can see my sin,
My hollow eyes, and oh,
My deathly pallid skin.

When silently he takes his leave
I am left with his child,
Growing in my belly
for I have been so defiled.

WILLINGLY

You gave yourself willingly to me
Feeling your life drip away,
And all the transfusions,
And all the wild notions,
Did nothing to keep me away.

You gave yourself willingly to me
Knowing what was to come,
And all your laments,
And all your repents,
Remember, it was you who
succumbed.

You gave yourself willingly to me
No matter how great the pain,
And all of your tears,
And all of your fears,
In the end had all been in vain.

You gave yourself willingly to me
Right up until your dying breath,.
And all of your grace,
And your gentle embrace,
Make me honoured
to be part of your death

TEARS

The tears of anguish
I have cried,
Neath the shade
of the yew,
By many a graveside.

But of all the tears
That I have shed,
None pained me more,
Than those I cry
Now you are laid to rest.

Shadow

Shadow on the street,
Stirs something deep in me,
Like words of love and loss
That only I can feel.

The shadow at my window
Mirrors my dark heart,
And beckons me to follow
Like a beacon in the dark.

Shadow in my chamber
By dawn you'll be gone,
But if only for tonight,
A taste of you is all I want.

Shadow on my heart
Where you lead I will follow,
Until I too become
A dark foreboding shadow.

REFLECTIONS

Within the limpid pool,
I see more than you
could ever hope to see,
Shallow mortal I see all.

Yet with your vanity
looking glass
You catch only a glimpse,
But I see in murky waters
All that I've become,
And in your eyes
I see your hopes and dreams.

I see beyond your
Painted aging visage,
Yet you see nothing of my soul.
All this illusion and delusion,
Is shattered with one kiss,
For just one is all it takes.

That's all it ever takes
To see beyond this realm
To see there's more
beyond the jaded image,
that's staring coldly
Back at you,
From within your looking glass.

Hell's Fire

If Hell's fire burns half as bright
As the flame dancing in your eyes,
The Devil can take my soul
For I fear I can no longer bear this
life.

So, if damned and cursed is my fate
Until time itself comes to an end,
Then beautiful demon take my hand,
And let me into hell descend.

My Weeping Heart

My weeping heart
Cries tears of blood
Since you left me all alone,
And every little sound
Chills me to the bone.

The creaking gate,
A scurrying mouse,
The branches,
Tapping on the windowpane,
The groaning of this house.

Every whisper from outside
That's carried on the wind,
The dripping tap,
The thunderclap,
All remind me of my sin.

But it in the end 'twas either
Me or you, and I chose I,
And drank your sweet blood
Knowing all along I would live,
And you would surely die

And now for eternity
It's your suffering I can hear,
Every groan, and every creek,
and every stormy night
Is a memory of your fear.

The rain and wind against
My bedroom windowpane,
The creaky door, tapping branches,
Are all a constant reminder
Of the choices I have made.

You were my one true love
And I threw it all away,
So, my heart shall cry
a thousand tears
In memory of that day.

Shadow on the Wall

Shadow on the wall,
Deathly, sinister, beyond this world,
Tall, and hunched,
Fingernails, long, and curled.
There's a howl deep within
That only I can hear.
And down your cheek,
A solitary tear.

Shadow on the wall
With your heart black as night,
A lonesome, shadow cast
In the pale moonlight.
There's a sorrow deep within,
A torment, an ache, a loss,
A harrowing burden,
Something, loved and lost

Shadow on the wall
Weary of the cross you bear,
I can feel your pain
Lingering in the air.
There's a heart deep within
That's been ripped apart,
An anguish from days long gone
Something, deep and dark.

Shadow on the wall
Pensive and foreboding,
Crepuscular and obscure,
Waiting to be invited in.
There's a lust deep within
Sinister and perverse,
Nefarious and threatening,
A vile, malevolent curse.

Shadow on the wall
Creature of the night,
I offer you my love,
My heart, my soul, my life.
There's a hunger deep within
That I alone can feed,
Take my hand, take my throat,
For you I willingly bleed.

LOVE

Love unrequited, forever I'm the beast,
Once I was beautiful, but now,
Violently I feast, as
Each night the hunger in me grows.

Longingly I search this land,
Oh, if only I could end this life, for
Vile and wretched I've become,
Every meal, a vagabond or whore.

Lascivious are my needs,
Eternal, and unending my lament,
Vilified, and outcast by those with whom,
Erstwhile I was content.

Lonely is this miserable path,
Obscure, and filled with pain.

So, Vampyre slayer, I pray dig deep,
Exhume my sorrowful remains.

Lift the lid and wield thy stake
Over my pitiful, undead, cadaver,
Vanquish the foe that lives in me,
End this unholy hunger now, and
forever.

GRIEF

What is the point
of this meagre existence,
with its unyielding apostasy?
The years grow ever crueller,
And the hunger ever stronger.
There's a void in me
that once was filled,
With joy and all life's riches:
The fleeting glance
of forbidden love,
The lingering touch
of my true love's kiss,
Long sunny days,
and summer haze,
That bring the heart such bliss.

But loss brings such suffering
And grief is hard to bear.
What man can bear the anguish

Of his family torn asunder.
When all the world
Comes crashing down
And joie de vivre is no more,
Then only torment fills his soul
And the void grows ever deeper.

Consumed by grief,
wrack'd with guilt,
A man takes any comfort.
But eternal torment,
relentless anguish,
And a yearning
beyond compare. –
Unquenchable thirst,
And unsatiated lust
Are a costly price to pay
But pay it I surely must.

So, I am destined
To walk this earth,
Hiding in the shadows
Of the witching hour.
From dusk till dawn
Is my domain,
Enter at your peril.
For this world has taken so much,
And owes me yet, far more
Than it can ever pay.
So, from Hesperus
to Phosphorous
I will stake my claim.

Senses

*Can you hear the children of the
night?
Their music filled with passion,
Each note carried high upon the
wind
Is a melancholy confession.
Each one seeking forgiveness,
For their putrid, festering soul,
Hoping for a saviour,
An inkling of hope.*

*Can you taste their disillusionment
As it lingers on the air?
The wretched hopelessness,
Their pitiful despair,
Their voices crying out,
For a saviour or redeemer,
Knowing there is no salvation
For such infernal creatures.*

Can you see the clouds
Hanging heavy in the sky?
The storm they are bringing
Carries the tears they have cried,
They weep for days long gone
Before they were damned to walk in
shade,
Their tears a bitter reminder
Of love, long since decayed.

Can you smell the dank aroma
As it taints the warm night air?
Rotten, pungent, fetid,
A vile and rancid prayer.
Every word tinged
Like the dying petals of the rose,
Defiled by their very existence,
An embryonic ghost.

Can you touch the horror
Lamented in their sad lullaby?
Can you see the hideous face
Of happier days gone by?
Can you feel the terror
Hidden in every lyric, every tune?
Do you remember still,
The world before the tomb?

Damned

Take this life - life be damned,
For it's no life at all
When I am condemned to be little
more
Than a shadow on your wall.

I will take all you are, all you will
ever be,
I will tear your world apart
Leave you crying, demanding,
wanting more
All alone in the dark.

Is this the life -the life you truly
want?
To be eternally damned.
To be a flicker, a fleeting glance,
A shadow on the wall.

I have walked this earth a thousand times
Tasted every corner of this world,
Left plague and death in my wake,
Wept over many a pretty girl.

I have taken numerous lovers,
Men and women have become my brides,
I have left them decaying and broken,
Carried away on windswept nights.

Oh, the travelling I have done for you
Through many treacherous lands.
I have crossed oceans of time to find you,[1]
For destiny holds my purpose in her hands.

I have learned much from all from my failures,
Simply to be worthy of your time,
To walk with you beside me on moonlit shores,
Where our words cannot be denied.

Where dear one, we can build our castles [2]
High above us in the winter air,
And spend the night together as lovers,
This is my one and only prayer.

For you alone I would share the sunrise
See it rise one last time upon the sea.
For you alone I would scorch my wicked soul
If you would walk the night with me.

Invite me in or step outside my love,
Walk with me into the twilight haze.
Take my hand and share my world
tonight,
And we shall kiss the stars, that
dance out over the bay.

So, when the sun does rise in a
glorious blaze of colour,
Hold my heart as I burn for you with
lust,
For by your side, I accept my fate,
For in the end, everything turns to
dust.

---

1 - From the 1992 Movie Bram Stoker's Dracula Directed by Frances Ford Coppola, (American Zoetrope, Osiris Film) distributed by Columbia Pictures
2 - From Bram Stoker's Dracula chapter 5

INSPIRATIONS

While the poetry in this book is solely my own work, there can be little doubt that some poems have more obvious influences than others. These include the following:

Vampyre - Hammer House of Horror
Countess Erzbet - Countess Elizabeth/Erzbet Bathory
Blood Lust - Jack the Ripper
Music - Shakespeare
Whitby Bay, Lucille, Slayer, Damned - Bram Stoker, Whitby Bay by Elisa Lo Presti (Red Right Hand Workshop), Bram Stokers Dracula Directed by Frances Ford Coppola.
Your Touch - John William Polidori
Shadow on the Wall - F W Murnau (Nosferatu a Symphony of Horror 1922)

The Kiss is solely mine and was inspired by the witch's fivefold kiss. It was adapted by Taloch Jameson for use on the album Nuada by the Dolmen, which was also inspired by the Vampyre. The Kiss became the title Track.

Lightning Source UK Ltd.
Milton Keynes UK
UKHW051122260123
415993UK00012B/114